THE NIGHT, THE CITY, AND MISS THING

ANGELA CAROLE BROWN

HAIKU HOUSE

The Night, the City, and Miss Thing

H A I K U   H O U S E

Book Jacket Design by Angela Carole Brown
Cover Photograph of Miss Thing by John Grab
Author Photo, a pandemic selfie

Published by Haiku House
ISBN-13: 978-1-7337453-3-8

Visit the author at:
www.angelacarolebrown.com

Visit the Orchestre Surreal at:
www.theorchestresurreal.com

All of Angela's books can be found at:
www.amazon.com/author/angelacarolebrown

This is a damned true story, Johnny

THE NIGHT, THE CITY, AND MISS THING

The story you are about to read takes place just after the turn of the Millennium, in the most torrid, sultry city in the world. So, get your strap-on fastened tight. You're in for a bumpy ride. Cue the Bernard Herrmann.

The street is dark and wet. Straight out of *The Third Man*. Moody, too (although allusions to the 3rd-M probably make that unnecessary to qualify). I'm a sensualist. I can imbue mood onto any canvas in a film-noir-pulp-fiction heartbeat. You know the scene. Streetlamps refract their light against the glistening pavement in circles here and there like stage lights. Mysteries hide in the shadows. But otherwise there is no one and nothing around me. Only my tiny 2-cylinder foreign job, making its way 'round midnight across the emptiness of downtown Los Angeles—but pronounced with a hard G, like the shamuses of old: "**Loss AN-geh-leees**"—the whooshing sighs of tread on rain-drenched asphalt, though the rain itself has stopped. Not even the homeless, of which there is a copious population in these parts, seems to be in the vicinity of this stretch of brick tenement buildings and corrugated metal pull-downs, in movie black & white. They've all seemed to find their way underground, I imagine, until the sidewalks dry. Is there such an underground? Or are they merely camouflaged against the mud-colored landscape of industrial drab, invisible but present? The city is asleep by every indication of my surroundings. I pull up to the address on my yellow notepad, and park directly across the street from my destination. I see no other cars, which means I'm the first one here. And I don't intend on getting out until I see a familiar car, a familiar face.

Damn Ross for this. There's always a White Rabbit adventure he's got us going on, and this particular one feels especially dubious. After all, I'm dressed head-to-toe like the mutant offspring of RuPaul and Norma Desmond. It's my own creation, The Fabulous Miss Thing, an arguably self-governing alter ego that allows me carte blanche on the stuff I could never dare as Angela. The uniform is a platinum pageboy wig, teased and poofed out so voluminously that I can barely fit in my car without grazing it on the ceiling. Black satin bustier that shows an ample bosom, and which is even bosom-ier when I'm in the seated position. I can literally rest my head on my boobs if I've a mind to. The only thing covering any portion of boobage is the white satin Miss America sash that goes over the shoulder and across the décolletage that says "Miss Thing" in elementary school cursive glitter-glue. A floor-length black latex skirt, with train, that evokes Morticia Addams, whom I've always longed to evoke. Leopard-spot platform hooker strappies that make me drag queen tall. And finally, black satin opera gloves with claw-long, blood-red press-on nails affixed to the fingertips. My proudest accomplishment in the area of drag queen chic.

I was mistaken for one once, wearing this very getup, as I attempted to apply my false eyelashes in the mirror of the women's room at Club Largo. They didn't have a dressing room for us, so it all had to be done right there in relative public, when a woman walked in and stopped dead at the door. She wore mom jeans on her petite frame like a defiant housewife, clutching her purse like it was a chastity belt, and draping disapproval over her shoulders like a diva's velvet cape. I loved her instantly.

"I don't think you're in the right room," came the tight-lipped warning, underscored with her disgust that I, penis-owner that I MUST have been, would have the gall to choose the women's room for my sartorial transformation.

I responded in the lowest-register voice I could muster, but with an attempted sass only drag queens truly know how to muster: "Honey, we're in West Hollywood. Every room is the right room."

Fuck 'em if they can't take a joke.

I presently stare out of my car window, which is fogging up because I insist on talking to myself: "Damn you, Ross! Why do you drag me to these freak fests, then don't even have the nerve to show up on time?"

I adjust my wig, and check my makeup in the rear view mirror. *Not a bad-lookin' dame,* I think to myself. I'll put on my tiara after I exit the car. Not enough room in this tiny cabin.

Twenty minutes pass. I don't own a cell

phone. Finally I give up waiting and exit the car. I look around, darting eyes this way and that, shake everything out, adjust my boobs inside the bustier, and place the tiara on my head, but am prepared to wield it as a weapon should the need arise.

I hasten across the street, holding my Morticia train in my left hand to keep it from getting wet, and I run across as fast as my platform stilettos will allow. The banging on the door lasts longer than I'm comfortable with, and I fear waking up the sleeping shopping carts that may be hovering near after all. This part of town is adjacent to Skid Row, and not exactly the Brewery District either, but some sort of limbo Purgatory in between. Artists may very well have lofts here, but I've seen neither hide nor hint of an artist yet. Only my own scared, bouffanted shadow. Why didn't I hitch a ride with Ross? Or Dan? Or Liz? My partners in crime this evening, if they ever decide to show up. But then again, we'd all be late if I'd done that.

My banging finally results in an open door, opened so violently I'm almost throttled with it. The woman on the other side looks like someone Warhol would've groomed. If anyone is destined to escort me down a witching-hour rabbit hole, this aging, avuncular Candy Darling lookalike is it. Ms. Darling was one of Warhol's protégés. A transgender icon, at once gentile and severe, who starred in several of his movies. Sure enough, she leads me down a narrow, unlit staircase to a darkened Orphean lair, startlingly evocative of Warhol's infamous Factory. She's charming, and chatty in that airy-wisp-of-a-sigh way that says *but I'm tortured*, and I apologize for the tardiness of my mates, swearing to her that they must be shortly behind me, only to be told they're already here; I'm the one who's late, it turns out. Why hadn't I seen their cars outside? I never do get that answer.

As I follow my Darling through a maze of partitions and strangely lit cubbyholes and cubicles, shadows falling like cool mist, we finally arrive at the bowels. A space with film cameras and lights. A set whose centerpiece is a round, ultra king-sized bed draped in bordello pink. A bevy of sofas on the set's periphery, meant to create a kind of waiting lounge area. And people. People everywhere. Behind the cameras. Holding up boom mics and slate clapper boards. Standing around with giant makeup brushes in their hands. Lounging on the sofas. And the hostess herself, Dr. Susan Block, a brassy blond who is actually a real life bona fide psychologist, even if her claim-to-fame is a sex talk show for public access TV, sprawled across the bed draped in little more than her pet boa constrictor.

My comely escort promptly disappears, as Ross and Dan wave me over to where they're sitting on a cluster of ottomans in the waiting lounge.

For some inexplicable reason, when my mouth opens an English accent comes out. I tend to do that. It's the silly in me, and I actually have a pretty natural ear for it. I must be feeling the need to be even more incognito than my Miss Thing armor renders me. And true to nutty form, neither Ross nor Dan even blinks an eye, as the world we've created for ourselves is a strange one indeed, as befitting the name of our organization, the Orchestre

Surreal. Dan jumps right on the Brit thing, and Ross simply chuckles.

"Where the hell have you brought us to?" I ask, through clenched teeth.

Imagine that, though, sounding like a whispering, spitting Helen Mirren.

There is a smattering of other guests sitting on sofas, and a few pairs seem to be having sex. Wait, what? Am I seeing that right? It's awfully dark in here, but I swear coitus is happening all around me.

"Yeah, I really didn't know what to expect, to be honest," Ross whispers back. "But it'll be fun. Just go with it. We're here to promote the Ford show. Let's just stay focused on that."

I sit, vowing to cooperate, and stare at my comrades. A smile creeps. Dangerous Dan is a wild beast of a fellow, who decks himself out in red and gold satin fighter shorts and a Viking helmet. He has an astonishing singing voice, and an even more astonishing, larger-than-life personality and sense of humor. He dubs himself the opera singer with the lethal stinger, or the singing Viking with the destructive striking, or the Karate Pavarotti. In a word, he's an opera singer who moonlights as an MMA fighter. At least his alter ego does. I do think he actually does walk through his life speaking in rhyme. He's far nuttier than any of Miss Thing's antics, and he always steals the show with his bang up talent.

Ross's alter ego is Elvis Schoenberg, the musical miscegenation of the King of Rock, Elvis Presley, and the King of Early 20th-Century Dodecaphonic Music, Arnold Schoenberg.

You heard that right, Palooka.

In fact, of all our repertoire, the one piece that actually IS that exact marriage is a 12-tone version of *Blue Suede Shoes* ... sung by Miss Thing ... in German ... well, pseudo-fake-joke German ... with a rap.

You can't make this stuff up!

And yet, though this madness comes from inside that brain, Ross is actually the most mild-mannered one of the group. But brilliant. I mean, brilliant this madcap jasper is. He's created a thirty-piece orchestra, as its sole orchestrator, arranger, conductor, lead man, and boss.

But it's not just any symphony orchestra, which, sorry to say, Joe, are just a dime a dozen. Elvis Schoenberg's Orchestre Surreal ain't proper like those other squares. It's a saucy tomato that's given Mr. Toad a run for his money. Here it is, in a nutshell. (Our *Blue Suede Shoes* has hopefully given some hint.) The Orchestre Surreal pushes against the boundaries of genre, and dares to suggest a world stripped of those borders, by presenting radically different artistic expressions and genres that, in Elvis Schoenberg's world, have every obligation to collide. Imagine Hendrix collaborating with Stravinsky. The Doors convening with Debussy. Nancy Sinatra in a Wagnerian opera. Unholy marriages that couldn't be more anointed under any other baton but our Elvis's. The result is a fearless deconstructing of known and unknown songs with the wit and whimsy of Spike Jones but the musical depth of Frank Zappa, with just a smidge of Juan Garcia Esquivel and Yma Sumac thrown in for good measure, while showcasing easily the wackiest wacky-savant orchestra of studio musicians in recent history. It actually does require a learned crowd to fully get Ross's thing, even with the sometime foray into the scatological. It's a marriage of high-brow and low-brow, to be sure. But we *are* about to appear on what seems to be some sort of porn set, so just how high-brow can we be?

Ross's ensemble is tux and tails, as per the conductor's uniform, but with zebra stripes of bright red and green. Leopard spotted cuffs. Gumby hairdo. Black, horn-rimmed specs. He's quite a fit and dapper gent, but you'd almost never know that to see him outfitted as Elvis.

"Where's Liz?" I suddenly think to ask.

And just as I ask it, she appears; cute little girl/woman, clad in her actual Catholic school uniform, with the skirt hemmed extra high, showing off a solid set of gams. Yes, she is all that, and a killer violinist to boot, who, of the string section members, was the only one willing to tag along on this shadows-and-fog Wonderland quest. But she's also clearly just as wigged out as I am about this cable access carnal circus, and expresses her concerns to Ross that whatever happens tonight her parents can never know about. Ross does his best to calm the women down. An added burden to being the ringleader.

I continue with my English accent, and

Ross dares me to commit fully. Susan Block doesn't know us from Adam; she has no idea if I really talk this way or not. Hell, count me in. How can it possibly be any more screwy than what we're already inside of?

As **Dr.** Susan speaks into a camera, she evokes a bit of Elvira in slinky style, except the words coming out of her mouth are damned smart. She's talking politics, and it turns out the doll's got a head for it.

She introduces her first guest, a gentleman dressed very like an Ivy League professor, who proceeds to read dirty poetry to a young woman dressed as Alice (she of the original rabbit hole) who does nothing but sit there.

Hmmmm. Can I apply for THAT job? It's all so *La Dolce Vita*. Or ... what's the other Fellini flick? The one about circus folk? ... *La Strada*. That's the one. Or Jodorowky's *Santa Sangre*. This scene is just kinky enough to be an absolute debauch! I'm talking *Caligula*, the Guccione cut.

But I digress. After the Professor and Alice finish their performance art, they join Dr. Susan and her snake on the big bed.

On this account, my bewigged head nearly explodes.

"We're not getting on that bed with that snake!" I spit into Ross's ear. Well, Judi Dench is spitting in his ear. For, even in my panic, I have fully committed to the Brit thing.

"Really? Come on. It'll be fun."

I have to give it to Ross (even though there is no way he's winning this one); he has the best attitude of anyone I know about leaping into unsure waters, and a kind of bravery I don't possess for traversing the unknown and the bizarre. It's precisely why he can create as brilliantly as he does. No one's told him, "you can't do that, Dutch!" Or if they have, Dutch ain't listenin'.

Well, the bizarre I've given into tonight. But I'm still not getting anywhere near a boa constrictor.

"I am NOT getting anywhere near a boa

constrictor!" I whisper, as the cameras roll on Dr. Suzy and her first guests.

We sit through a few other guests, all dubiously displaying their wares and various talents, much of which has some kind of sex angle.

"We don't have a sex angle," Dan says to Ross. "What are we doing here?"

"Trying to get an audience to our show!" Ross whispers, clearly betraying his annoyance, to the umpteenth person (well, just me, Dan, and Liz) who questions why we're here. The scoop of this cold-hearted business, and this cold-hearted town, is that the hustle has to go right alongside the art, or you're sunk. So here we are, paying our dues in the most extreme way the phrase could possibly mean.

Eventually it's our turn. Dr. Susan has been informed that her next guests will NOT be sharing a space with her snake, fornication might very well still be going on upon a nearby sofa, and the hostess herself seems warm and intelligent (easy to assume the worst, and the worst is what I have been assuming). Turns out, she's actually written for The Alternet and The Ecologist on civil liberties and freedom of speech. She's no dummy, I learn quickly. She just decided that being a "sexologist" was her calling.

We climb upon this prop bed, which is no

easy feat, considering the skin-tight getup I'm wearing. Plus, there are four of us, not counting Dr. Susan. And yes, I have continued with the English accent, and so the first question upon the cameras rolling is, "where are you from, Miss Thing?" When I answer "Compton," which is no joke, which is the absolute truth, but sounding like Kate Winslet, the whole room laughs. And we're off and running.

And, as fate would have it, Dr. Susan Block turns out to be an absolute dish to chat with! She enthusiastically tells her television audience all about our upcoming show at the Ford Amphitheatre, across the freeway from the Hollywood Bowl, and none too shabby a venue its own damn self. And she describes Ross's music as politically charged by the simple virtue of its strange-bedfellows juxtaposition of seemingly conflicting musical elements. She really does get us! And of course Dangerous Dan is making the whole room laugh with his Robin-Williams-on-speed quick wit. And so this cable access spot is actually working the way we need it to work. We're downright entertaining, I tell ya'. Unless, of course, no one's watching. And I can't say there isn't some part of me that's sorta hoping no one is. At least … no one I know. My prejudices are definitely winning.

Still, Miss Thing is having a wicked good time—at least the Edina & Patsy version is—while regaling stories with my compatriots about our upcoming show, whose plot, just as a by the by, involves gamma rays, aliens, and Miss Thing saving the planet.

Because ... you know ... why not?

Dr. Suzy keeps trying to get the skirts to show the audience a nipple or two, which neither of us is about to do, but we beg off with giggles and coyness instead of indignation. Because we're here. No place to be presenting as self-righteous when we're all sprawled out on a big-ass porn bed, and would, each one of us, be hauled off to Parker Center if the Law decided to raid the place. But yes, Dr. Suzy is certainly giving it her best shot at a sex angle between the broads, however futile, as this is what her show IS.

Ross talks about his vision for the orchestra, of laying the foundation for a new Avant Garde. Balls, this one is. Dan stands up on the bed and does an impromptu rendition of Puccini's *Nessun Dorma*, making the bed tip and bounce like the last hours of the Titanic. I do my promotional spiel, channeling Her Royal Highness: "We're venturing out into the daylight once again, my loyal subjects, therefore lock up your clown cars! Friends and foes alike, flood the palace with your love and/or to-MAH-toes. We're not picky." And Liz gives us all a little sampling from her violin. Meanwhile, Dr. Suzy comes awfully close to licking Liz's bow.

The Doc is playful and frisky tonight, and she wants us to be playful and frisky too. And we're only willing to go so far, which she can't possibly be pleased about, but what's a girl to do. It's certainly a surreal twenty minutes, as I keep one eye forever cocked to make sure that damned snake is nowhere slithering.

At the very least, our spot does manage to include all the pertinent details of our subversive vaudeville-on-acid spectacle, aptly named *Symphony of the Absurd*.

Now, this begs pause.........................

You see, there came a point, within the years of being involved with this strange endeavor, where I think we all realized we'd stepped into something that might just take us to another dimension. And there's always the tease of danger whenever flight is taken and horizons are breached. Absurd is most certainly a part of what we've invited with this genre-obliterating, no-holds-barred musical universe Ross has created.

As unsure as the twists and turns may sometimes be, there is honestly no greater thrill than to be involved in something so unique, so singular, so seductive. After all, crazy promotional efforts like tonight's John Waters odyssey aside, Elvis Schoenberg, in the form of mild-mannered Ross Wright from Laguna Beach, California, and his fecund Orchestre Surreal are stripping away the barriers of cultural, generational, and artistic divide, just as surely as we are also mischievously riffing on hermaphrodism, fossil fuels, and foot fetishes.

As the director calls cut on our segment of *The Dr. Susan Block Show*, and I secretly wonder if it'll make the cut of my résumé, I ponder the mask I wear as The Fabulous Miss Thing. It's certainly an E-ticket to wild adventures, as Angela would never be caught dead in a place like this, or would leave immediately upon discovery. And honestly, it would be my loss. Because, there is nothing duller than a meticulously planned life without the wild fringes to remind us we are no cookie-cutter emblems of humanity; but merely … beautifully … humanity. In all its thousand shapes, timbers, tempos, and tangs. But what's even more poignant—if poignancy can be had by a platinum-wig-and-tiara-wearing, pageant-sash-donning cartoon character—is that Miss Thing is also the E-ticket to infinite possibilities on stage.

As Angela, it's pretty awkward for me to try and "do" sexy for the crowd. Besides which, performance for me has never been about trying to sell my sexuality to an audience as a commodity. And even if that were important to me, being some mischievous, vampy Rita Hayworth or Dorothy Dandridge chimera is virtually impossible for me to conjure anyway, because it's just too distracting from being able to truly connect to a song. Frankly, it renders a feeling of silliness because I don't buy it. And if I don't *buy* it, how on earth can I *sell* it?

Yet the minute the mask is on, the minute I am The Fabulous Miss Thing instead of Angela, replete with hyperbolic adjective as an integral part of the moniker, I am IT, and effortlessly. I can handle a gun with one gloved hand, and plant one straight on the kisser of any button man that dares come my way with the other. I can pickpocket a speakeasy dope fiend, and dry-gulch the bum while crooning my first torched note. And I can sport a fake British accent while hanging out with the lookers and lugs in the bowels of Bukowski's L.A. and dare anyone to call me out for my lunacy.

And none of Miss Thing's antics creates any distraction from owning *her* song. In fact, the antics are as much a part of the song as the adjective is to the name.

There is just something about the comforting respite of the shadows behind the mask that allows Angela to own that Vamp stamp, or even Crazy Lady, so completely that there is no possibility for rejection.

That is, after all ... IT. Isn't it?

Putting oneself out there in a giant, unrepentant way, whether as Femme Fatale, Clown, or Diva (all three of which are Miss Thing at any given moment), leaves one wide open for a .38 slug to the heart.

Angela's couldn't take it. She'd much rather be the ego that is stripped down to the bare knuckles, operating merely as conduit, so the art itself shines. As for Miss Thing, not only can her heart take rejection, but she is so larger-than-life, so seizing the world by its

Misters, that rejection isn't even an option.

This last thought stops me in my existential stilettoed tracks.

Is it actually possible there are lessons for Angela to learn from The Fabulous Miss Thing? Or is it perfectly all right that Miss Thing is one phenomenon, gale force who will be reckoned with, while Angela is simply another, preferring to give the floor to the work itself? And that each has its place in the world of art and expression?

As an official five is called, for cameras to get reloaded and sets to get moved around, and that damned snake seems to be back in the picture, we all climb down from the giant fuchsia bed. Me, faster than anyone, almost losing my wig. Dr. Susan thanks us for joining her. My comrades and I sign release forms, shimmy off the flop sweat, and say our most heartfelt goodbyes. I glance around to see if I can wave a distanced "see ya" to my breakable Candy Darling. But like all the other mysteries that lurk in these musty drapes, she's nowhere to be found.

I feel a bit as if I've been zapped by one of those 1950's black-&-white hypno-wheels that's always accompanied by the eerie tremolo of a Theremin, followed by the haunting monotone promise: *You'll remember nothing of this once you hear the SNAP of the finger.*

As my accomplices and I walk out of the vast downtown dive into the naked city of this wanton L.A. night (actually, deep into the dark early morning by this point), our shadows tower and loom against a far wall at stark expressionistic angles. I fully expect Orson Welles and Joseph Cotton to come peering out from around a corner in their dusky fedoras, and for the sound of a tragic tenor saxophone to growl and sigh its nocturne cry.

The appropriately glistening streets have never been more appropriate, as the prisms of refracted light from the streetlamps in the here-and-there rain puddles threaten to hypnotize us into thinking this has all been a fever dream.

The rain suddenly returns, washing away

the whiskeyed breath of Raymond Chandler's

hardboiled town. And with the flick of her

press-on nails, The Fabulous Miss Thing hops

into her cheeky little sports car and drives off

into the sunrise.

Yes, I CAN magically morph my old

Toyota Tercel jalopy into Angelyne's* hot pink

Corvette if I believe it enough. This is, after all,

the city of stardust and dreamers.

I never even look back to see the exhaust

fumes from Elvis' 1965 Ford Ranchero Classic,

---

* Angelyne is probably only known to Angelenos for a series of iconic
pin-up billboards that plastered the city throughout the 1980's. She did
get some minor movie and television work from it. Some 40 years
later, she can still be seen driving around LA in her trademark peekaboo
outfits, brassy platinum hair, and hot pink Corvette.

as he and the rest of my **confrères** skid away to

their various outer limits of the Southland.

And like all great love stories, one more bit

of Surreal gets checked off a list that apparently

plans to go on … and on … and deliciously on.

Angela Carole Brown, AKA The Fabulous Miss Thing, is a 2018 recipient of the North Street Book Prize in Literary Fiction for her novel *Trading Fours*, and the SoulWord Magazine Poetry Prize for her single poem "Cotton Candy." She is also the author of the novel *The Assassination of Gabriel Champion*, the memoir *The Kidney Journals: Memoirs of a Desperate Lifesaver*, the poetry collections *Bones* and *Viscera*, the 100-word story collection *Aleatory on the Radio*, and the award-winning videobook *The Richest Girl in the World*. She writes the blog Bindi Girl Chronicles. She has been on the L.A. music scene for over three decades as a singer, songwriter, and recording artist, has produced several albums of music in the genres of jazz and folk, and is the lead female vocalist in Elvis Schoenberg's Orchestre Surreal, which won the L.A. Music Award for "Best Rock Opera" in 2004 for their show *Symphony of the Absurd*.